A Seder for Tu B'Shevat

By
Harlene Winnick Appelman
Jane Sherwin Shapiro
Illustrated by
Chari R. McLean

KAR-BEN
PUBLISHING

To my parents. —H.W.A.

Acknowledgements
Poem, p. 22 *Unfair* by Bobbi Katz, from *Time To Shout: Poems by You,*
    Scholastic Book Service, 1973.
Music, pp. 29–30 courtesy of Velvel Pasternak, Tara Publications.
Music, p. 31 used by permission of Cherry Lane Music Co., Inc.

KAR-BEN PUBLISHING, INC.
A division of Lerner Publishing Group
241 First Avenue North
Minneapolis, MN 55401 U.S.A.
800-4KARBEN

Website address: www.karben.com

Library of Congress Cataloging-in-Publication Data

Appelman, Harlene Winnick
    A Seder for Tu B'Shevat.
    Summary: Describes the celebration of the Jewish arbor day,
  Tu B'Shevat, and explains its history.
    ISBN: 0–930494–39–3 (pbk. : alk. paper)
    1. Tu B'Shevat—Juvenile literature. [1. Tu B'Shevat] I. Shapiro, Jane.
  II. McLean, Chari, ill. III. title.
  BM695.T9A66 1984
  296.4'39   84-25101

Manufactured in the United States of America
7 8 9 10 11 12 – JR – 08 07 06 05 04 03

INTRODUCTION

The Tu B'Shevat seder is an old/new tradition. The 16th century Kabbalists (who also brought us the Friday evening service to welcome Shabbat) gathered Erev Tu B'Shevat for singing, dancing, and fruit-tasting. But the custom was lost for many centuries among the Jewish communities of the west.

Winter is a wonderful time for a celebration, especially an affirmation of the coming of spring and the renewal of life.

The seder we present is adaptable in many different settings—schools, synagogue groups, chavurot, families. It includes the history of the holiday, songs, blessings, stories and, of course, eating and drinking. The basic readings and blessings take about half an hour. With additional readings, songs, and time for discussion, the seder will take an hour. We have avoided designating ''leader'' and ''reader'' parts, so that you may tailor the readings to the size and age of your group. Many of the stories and marginal comments and activities may be read silently or skipped.

Do involve children in the preparations. They may make wall hangings, place cards, decorations, set the table, help peel and cut up the fruit. To keep the attention of very young children, hide a walnut at the beginning of the seder. At the end, the one who finds it receives a prize! You may also wish to serve cookies and cakes or even a light supper in conjunction with the seder. Check a siddur for additional food blessings.

There are more activities at the back of the book—to make your TuB'Shevat a memorable holiday

—H.W.A.
—J.S.

PREPARING FOR THE SEDER

The table should be set with a pretty cloth and decorated with flowers, branches, and leaves. Candles (try scented ones) add a festive touch.

PLACE SETTINGS

Each person will need:
Plate (paper or plastic are easiest)
Fork or toothpicks for fruit-tasting
Flower pot or paper cup filled with potting soil
Wine cup
Napkin
Tu B'Shevat Haggadah

WINE

You will need bottles or carafes of red and white wine or grape juice—enough to serve each person four cups.

SEDER FRUIT PLATES

You will need three platters of fruit, as follows:

Fruits with an inedible shell (at least 5):

Tangerine	*Grapefruit*
Kiwi	*Coconut*
Walnut	*Peanut*
Pomegranate	*Almond*
Pistachio	*Orange*

Fruits with an inedible pit or seed (at least 5):

Peach	*Plum*
Avocado	*Date*
Olive	*Cherry*
Apricot	*Mango*

Fruits which are edible inside and out (at least 5):

Grape	*Raisin*
Fig	*Cranberry*
Apple	*Pear*
Strawberry	*Carob*

Cut fruit into bite-size pieces ahead of time, so that your seder can proceed smoothly.

SEDER SEED PLATE

Prepare a platter of seed packets for planting. Choose herbs (parsley is fun to grow for the upcoming Passover seder), vegetables (tomatoes, cucumbers, lettuce), or flowers (marigolds, petunias). Place a few water pitchers around the table, so participants may water their seeds after planting.

At the beginning of the
seder, put a white carnation
or a stalk of celery in a glass
of water. Add red food
coloring. By the end of the
seder, you will see the
miracle of Tu B'Shevat.

When you think of a new year, what do you picture? Your birthday, your own special new year with candles and a cake? January 1, with noisemakers, party hats, and streamers? The beginning of the school year, with a new notebook, book bag, and lunch box? Or maybe Rosh Hashanah, with apples, honey, and the sound of the shofar.

Tu B'Shevat, the 15th day of the Hebrew month of Shevat, is another new year, the New Year of the Trees. In Hebrew, it is called Rosh Hashanah Le'Ilanot. Like other new years, Tu B'Shevat has a rich tradition of celebration.

The Hebrew letters Tet and Vav which spell Tu have a number value of 15. Tu B'Shevat means "the 15th of Shevat."

Tu B'Shevat falls in late January or early February. In many parts of the world, the ground is snow-covered, and birds have flown off to warmer spots. In Israel, however, where the holiday began more than 2000 years ago, the winter rains have tapered off, and the sap that brings food to the limbs of the tree starts to rise. Buds appear, and the land takes on a springtime glow. As nature comes to life, it feels like a new year.

The Kabbalists, a group of Jewish mystics living in Israel in the 16th century, created a Seder for Tu B'Shevat. They gathered in the evening around a beautiful table decorated with sweet-smelling flowers and lovely candles. Long into the night, they sang, and talked, and ate.

Today, we gather as they did to study, sing, and celebrate the great miracle of trees.

How good it is that we have come together!

All sing:
Hinei mah tov u'mah na'im shevet achim gam yachad.

(Music p. 29)

FOUR QUESTIONS FOR TU B'SHEVAT

Why is this day different from all other days?

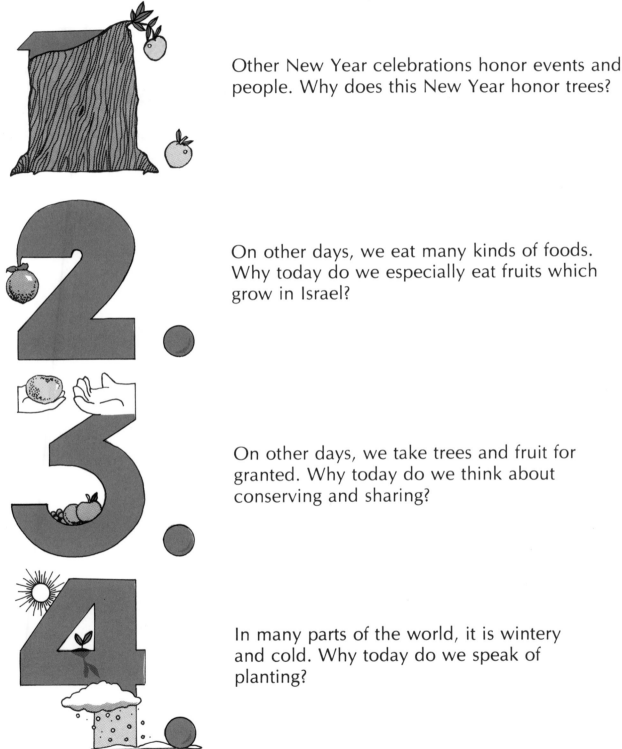

Other New Year celebrations honor events and people. Why does this New Year honor trees?

On other days, we eat many kinds of foods. Why today do we especially eat fruits which grow in Israel?

On other days, we take trees and fruit for granted. Why today do we think about conserving and sharing?

In many parts of the world, it is wintery and cold. Why today do we speak of planting?

As we answer these questions, we will learn about the holiday we have come to celebrate.

THE FIRST CUP OF WINE

We begin our seder for Tu B'Shevat, as we begin all holiday celebrations, with the drinking of wine or grape juice. Before the seder is over, we will drink four cups. Each cup reminds us of a season in Israel.

The first cup is entirely white wine or juice, reminding us of winter, when nature is asleep. The earth is barren, sometimes snow-covered, awaiting the rebirth of spring.

We join in the blessing over the wine, and give thanks that we can be together in celebration.

בָּרוּךְ אַתָּה יְיָ אֱלֹהֵינוּ מֶלֶךְ הָעוֹלָם, בּוֹרֵא פְּרִי הַגָּפֶן:

Baruch atah adonai, eloheinu melech ha'olam, borei p'ri hagafen.

Blessed are You, Lord our God, King of the Universe, who creates the fruit of the vine.

בָּרוּךְ אַתָּה יְיָ אֱלֹהֵינוּ מֶלֶךְ הָעוֹלָם, שֶׁהֶחֱיָנוּ וְקִיְּמָנוּ וְהִגִּיעָנוּ לַזְּמַן הַזֶּה:

Baruch atah adonai, eloheinu melech ha'olam, shehecheyanu, v'kiyemanu, v'higianu laz'man hazeh.

Blessed are You, Lord our God, King of the Universe, who has granted us life and brought us together in this season of our joy.

THE SEDER PLATES

On the table are three plates of fruit, each of them different. During our seder, we will taste fruits from each plate, so we may notice and appreciate their differences.

The first plate has fruits with a peel or shell that cannot be eaten, such as:

Orange, Tangerine, Grapefruit, Kiwi, Coconut, Peanut, Walnut, Almond, Pomegranate, Mango

Before we taste the fruit, we recite the bracha:

בָּרוּךְ אַתָּה יְיָ אֱלֹהֵינוּ מֶלֶךְ הָעוֹלָם, בּוֹרֵא פְּרִי הָעֵץ:

Baruch atah adonai eloheinu melech ha'olam borei p'ri ha'etz.

Blessed are You, Lord our God, King of the Universe, who creates the fruit of trees.

(All share the fruit.)

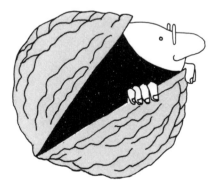

The Rabbis have taught us that people's personalities differ as fruits do. Do you know anyone who has a "shell?" A native born Israeli is called a sabra, after a cactus fruit that is hard on the outside and sweet on the inside. Can you guess why?

1. WHY TODAY DO WE HAVE A NEW YEAR JUST FOR TREES?

Certain mitzvot in the Torah make it very important to know the age of trees.

The Torah requires farmers to give a tithe (one tenth) of all crops grown during a given year to the priests of the Holy Temple. Tu B'Shevat marked the beginning of the year for tithing trees.

The Torah also says that we may not eat the fruit of a tree until the fourth year after it has been planted. Tu B'Shevat figures into this calculation as well.

In addition to these practical reasons for celebrating the birthday of trees, Tu B'Shevat celebrates the Jewish people's love of trees.

In the Talmud, we learn that when a new baby was born, the parents planted a cedar tree for a boy and a cypress tree for a girl. The children cared for their trees, and when they grew up and were ready to be married, branches from the two trees were used to make the pillars of the chuppah, the marriage canopy.

By planting trees, people showed they believed in a future for their children, who would grow up enjoying the fruit, shade, breeze, and beauty provided by trees.

Many years ago in Israel, there lived a righteous man whose name was Honi. One day, Honi saw an old man planting a carob tree. His grandchild was helping him. Honi laughed. ''Foolish man,'' he said, ''do you think you will still be alive to eat the fruit of this tree?''

The old man replied, ''I found trees in the world when I was born. My grandparents planted them for me. Now I am planting for my grandchildren.''

Weary from the heat of the day, Honi retired to a shady spot for a nap. But the short nap became a sleep of 70 years, and when he awakened, he did not know that his hair had turned as white as snow. He was surprised to see a full-grown carob tree and an elderly man picking its fruit. ''Are you the man who planted the tree?'' Honi asked.

''No,'' the old man replied. ''My grandfather planted it for me.''

THE SECOND CUP OF WINE

The second cup of wine is darker. We pour a bit of red wine into the white. Watch it change colors.

In Israel, as spring approaches, the sun's rays begin to thaw the frozen earth. Gradually the land changes its colors from white to red, as pink and white cyclamens appear in the mountains.

Before we drink, we recite:

בָּרוּךְ אַתָּה יְיָ אֱלֹהֵינוּ מֶלֶךְ הָעוֹלָם, בּוֹרֵא פְּרִי הַגָּפֶן:

Baruch atah adonai eloheinu melech ha'olam borei p'ri hagafen.

Blessed are You, Lord our God, King of the Universe, who creates the fruit of the vine.

Now we choose fruits from the second plate, fruits with pits or seeds that cannot be eaten, such as:

Peach, Plum, Avocado, Date, Olive, Cherry, Apricot, Mango

Let us recite the bracha:

בָּרוּךְ אַתָּה יְיָ אֱלֹהֵינוּ מֶלֶךְ הָעוֹלָם, בּוֹרֵא פְּרִי הָעֵץ:

Baruch atah adonai eloheinu melech ha'olam, borei p'ri ha'etz.

Blessed are You, Lord our God, King of the Universe, who creates fruit of the trees.

(All share the fruit.)

Did you know that a steady wind blowing from or direction may bend a tree, and that uneven light w cause it to grow crooked? But a tree usually gro straight because that is the best way for it to grow. I likely to live longer because its leaves have more ro to stretch towards the sun. Do you think a person is a tree?

2. WHY TODAY DO WE ESPECIALLY EAT FRUITS THAT GROW IN ISRAEL?

After the Temple was destroyed, and the Jews were forced to leave the land of Israel, the original purpose of Tu B'Shevat was lost. The laws of planting and tithing crops did not apply outside of Israel. But the holiday was preserved as a symbol of the love of the Jewish people for their land.

It became a custom to eat fruits that grow in the Holy Land—almonds, dates, olives, figs, carob, and pomegranates.

The Kabbalists created a formal Tu B'Shevat celebration modeled after the Passover Seder. Their Haggadah, called *Pri Etz Hadar, The Fruit of the Goodly Tree,* contained readings about trees from the Bible and the Talmud. They ate 15 different kinds of fruits, nuts, and grains, and drank four cups of wine.

In modern times, Tu B'Shevat has taken on new meaning. With the rebirth of the State of Israel, trees have become the symbol of rebuilding the land. When the early pioneers came to Palestine 100 years ago, the land was barren from centuries of wars and neglect. They planted trees and made the land bloom again.

Let us sing a song the Israeli pioneers sang while they planted:

> *Artzah alinu, artzah alinu, artzah alinu. (2)*
> *K'var charashnu v'gam zaranu (2)*
> *Aval od lo katzarnu. (2)*   (Music p. 29)

We have come up to the land, we have tilled the soil, and sown the seeds, but we have yet to harvest our crop.

While hiking in Israel, it is fun to look for different kinds of trees.

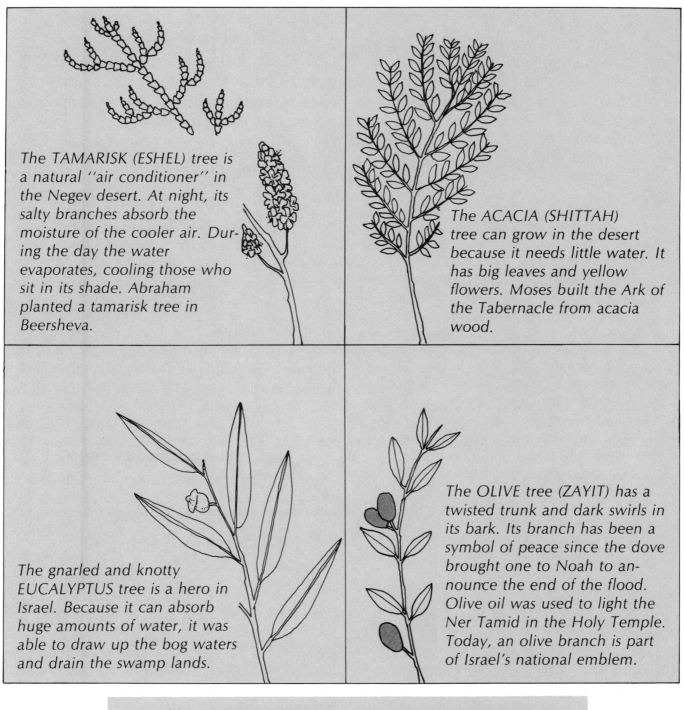

The TAMARISK (ESHEL) tree is a natural "air conditioner" in the Negev desert. At night, its salty branches absorb the moisture of the cooler air. During the day the water evaporates, cooling those who sit in its shade. Abraham planted a tamarisk tree in Beersheva.

The ACACIA (SHITTAH) tree can grow in the desert because it needs little water. It has big leaves and yellow flowers. Moses built the Ark of the Tabernacle from acacia wood.

The gnarled and knotty EUCALYPTUS tree is a hero in Israel. Because it can absorb huge amounts of water, it was able to draw up the bog waters and drain the swamp lands.

The OLIVE tree (ZAYIT) has a twisted trunk and dark swirls in its bark. Its branch has been a symbol of peace since the dove brought one to Noah to announce the end of the flood. Olive oil was used to light the Ner Tamid in the Holy Temple. Today, an olive branch is part of Israel's national emblem.

Rabbi Nachman of Bratslav composed this hiking poem:

Master of the Universe
Grant me the ability to be alone.
May it be my custom to go outdoors each day
Among the trees and grass, among all growing things.
And there may I enter into prayer
To talk with the One I belong to.

Do you ever think about the many things trees do for us? They:

Provide fruit and lumber
Protect from dust storms
Give shade from the hot sun
Reduce noise levels
Drain swamps
Prevent soil erosion
Lend beauty to the landscape

NATURAL CURES

For indigestion,
  chew parsley.
For a cold,
  drink camomile tea.
For staying young,
  smell rosemary.
For blemishes,
  apply bruised leaves of
    watercress.
For strength,
  eat thyme.

Do you know anyone named Tamar or Oren? Many Jewish children are given Hebrew names of flowers and trees that bloom in Israel.

Tamar—Palm
Oren—Pine
Ilan—Tree
Shoshana—Lily
Alon—Oak
Vered—Rose
Dafna—Laurel

In 1901, the Jewish National Fund was created to raise money to buy back and cultivate the land of Israel. Since that time, blue and white tzedakah boxes have been distributed in Jewish homes all over the world, so that families might contribute to this effort.

The JNF has planted more than 140 million trees throughout Israel. Forests and parks have been established in honor of America's Bicentennial; to remember world heroes, such as Theodore Herzl, President John F. Kennedy, and Martin Luther King, Jr.; and in memory of the children of the Holocaust.

Eli Cohen was born in Egypt, but came to Israel in 1957. He became a secret agent and was sent to work in Syria. There he earned a position of trust among the Syrian officials. One day, he suggested to the Syrian army officers that their outposts on the Golan Heights were not secure. "Why not plant eucalyptus trees," he said. "They will hide your positions, shade the hot soldiers, and catch the breezes." The Syrians agreed.

In 1965, Eli Cohen was arrested and executed in Damascus as a spy. Two years later during the Six Day War, when Israeli forces took the Golan Heights, they were able to spot the Syrian outposts easily. They looked for the eucalyptus trees on the otherwise barren hills.

THE THIRD CUP

The third cup of wine is still darker. We fill our kiddush cups with red wine and add a dash of white wine. Watch the colors mix.

As summer arrives, the land of Israel becomes bright red. Tulips and red poppies burst forth and bloom. The ground becomes soft. The farmer turns over the earth and drops in the seeds. Water, sunshine, and time combine to create new life. Let us bless and drink together:

בָּרוּךְ אַתָּה יְיָ אֱלֹהֵינוּ מֶלֶךְ הָעוֹלָם, בּוֹרֵא פְּרִי הַגָּפֶן:

Baruch atah adonai eloheinu melech ha'olam, borei p'ri hagafen.

Blessed are You, Lord our God, King of the Universe, who creates the fruit of the vine.

We now taste the third plate of fruits. They are edible both inside and out, such as:

Grape, Raisin, Fig, Cranberry, Apple, Pear, Strawberry, Carob.

Let us recite the bracha:

בָּרוּךְ אַתָּה יְיָ אֱלֹהֵינוּ מֶלֶךְ הָעוֹלָם, בּוֹרֵא פְּרִי הָעֵץ:

Baruch atah adonai eloheinu melech ha'olam, borei p'ri ha'etz.

Blessed are you, Lord our God, King of the Universe, who creates the fruit of trees.

(All share the fruit.)

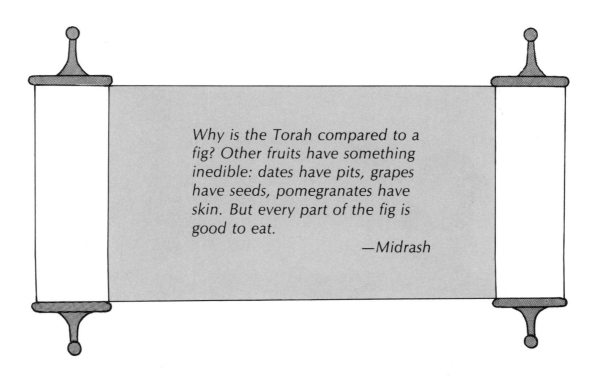

Why is the Torah compared to a fig? Other fruits have something inedible: dates have pits, grapes have seeds, pomegranates have skin. But every part of the fig is good to eat.

—Midrash

3. ON OTHER DAYS, WE TAKE TREES FOR GRANTED. WHY TODAY DO WE THINK ABOUT CONSERVING AND SHARING?

Trees were so important that Rabbi Yochanan Ben Zakkai taught: If you should be standing with a sapling in your hand when the Messiah arrives, first finish planting the tree, then go and greet the Messiah.

And the Bible tells us that when you make war against a city, you must not destroy its trees, because the trees of the field are your life.

The rabbis interpreted this as meaning that we should not be wasteful or destructive. Preventing forest fires, conserving energy that is needed to produce food, and recycling paper products are things we all can do to help our environment.

It doesn't seem fair
that a tree
that makes such
a good place
to hang your swing
and give shade
to people on hot days
and homes
to birds and chipmunks
could someday
get to be
a paper napkin.

Throughout history, the Jewish people have cared about those who are hungry. The laws of the Torah required farmers to leave the corners of their wheat, grape, and olive fields uncut. Harvesters could not pick up any stalks they had forgotten or dropped. These "leftovers" were reserved for the poor and the stranger to gather and eat. The Rabbis called the Torah *Etz Chayim,* the Tree of Life. Do these laws help explain why?

A *tzadik,* a righteous person, is often compared to the erez or cedar tree. The cedar grows straight, and so does a righteous person. The cedar's shade extends a great distance, just as a righteous person's good deeds help many others.

There is a Tu B'Shevat custom of giving *Ma'ot Perot,* money to needy families so they can buy fruit. We pass a tzedakah box around the table to collect coins for *Ma'ot Perot* and to plant trees in Israel.

As we participate in the mitzvah of tzedakah, let us sing a song together:

> *Tzadik katamar yifrach, yifrach*]
> *Tzadik katamar yifrach*] 2
> *K'erez ba'Levanon yisgeh (2)*
> *K'erez ba'Levanon yisgeh, yisgeh.* (Music p. 30)

> *The righteous shall flourish like a date palm; he shall grow tall as a cedar in Lebanon.*

Dates, which are nourishing and easy to dry and store, provide food for long journeys in the desert. It is probably because of this that Avshalom Feinberg had some dates in his pocket when he disappeared on his way to Egypt in 1917. Feinberg, a spy who worked for NILI, a group which opposed Turkish rule over Palestine, was on an important mission. It was assumed that he was captured and killed.

After the Israelis regained control of Gaza in 1967, an old Arab led some soldiers to Feinberg's grave. There stood a beautiful, tall date palm. It sprouted, perhaps, from the dates in Avshalom's pocket.

THE FOURTH CUP

Our fourth cup of wine is all red. Summer ends, the trees are filled with blossoming flowers, and the crops are growing tall as we reach autumn, the season of the harvest.

All recite:

בָּרוּךְ אַתָּה יְיָ אֱלֹהֵינוּ מֶלֶךְ הָעוֹלָם, בּוֹרֵא פְּרִי הַגָּפֶן:

Baruch atah adonai eloheinu melech ha'olam, borei p'ri hagafen.

Blessed are You, Lord our God, King of the Universe, who creates the fruit of the vine.

Instead of fruit, the fourth plate contains seeds. Later we will participate in the mitzvah of planting.

4. WHY ON A COLD AND WINTERY DAY DO WE TALK ABOUT SPRING PLANTING?

In Israel, Tu B'Shevat has become a day for planting trees. Children go out into the fields, valleys, and deserts and plant hundreds of saplings. Jewish children all over the world contribute money for tree-planting.

When the Israeli children plant their trees, they sing a song about the *shkediyah*, the almond tree, the first to bloom in the spring. Let's sing it, too:

Hashkediyah porachat, hashemesh gam zorachat
Tziporim al rosh kol gag m'vasrot et bo he'chag.
Tu B'Shevat higiyah, chag ha'ilanot. (2)   (Music p. 30)

The almond trees bloom under the sun's rays. The birds on the rooftops chirp a welcome. Tu B'Shevat, the holiday of trees, has arrived.

We are now ready to participate in the mitzvah of planting. Select some seeds from the packets on your table, place them in the soil, and water them.

Let's sing a folk-song about planting:

Inch by inch, row by row,
Gonna make this garden grow,
All it takes is a rake and a hoe
And a piece of fertile ground.

Inch by inch, row by row,
Someone bless these seeds I sow,
Someone warm them from below
'Til the rain comes tumblin' down.

Pullin' weeds and pickin' stones,
Man is made of dreams and bones
Feel the need to grow my own
'Cause the time is close at hand.

Grain for grain, sun and rain,
Find my way in nature's chain,
Tune my body and my brain
To the music from the land.

Plant your rows straight and long,
Temper them with prayer and song,
Mother Earth will make you strong
If you give her love and care.

Old crow watching hungrily,
From his perch in yonder tree,
In my garden I'm as free
As that feathered thief up there.

Inch by Inch...   (Music p. 31)

On seeing trees bloom for the first time in the spring, we say the following blessing:

בָּרוּךְ אַתָּה יְיָ
אֱלֹהֵינוּ מֶלֶךְ הָעוֹלָם,
שֶׁלֹּא חִסַּר בְּעוֹלָמוֹ דָּבָר,
וּבָרָא בוֹ בְּרִיּוֹת טוֹבוֹת
וְאִילָנוֹת טוֹבִים לְהַנּוֹת
בָּהֶם בְּנֵי אָדָם:

Baruch atah adonai
eloheinu melech ha'olam,
shelo chisar ba'olamo
davar, u'vara vo b'riot
tovot v'ilanot tovim l'hanot
bahem b'nai adam.

Blessed are You, Lord our God, King of the Universe, who has created beautiful creatures and trees in the world so that people may delight in them.

We end with the blessing of thanks for the food and wine we have shared:

בָּרוּךְ אַתָּה יְיָ אֱלֹהֵינוּ מֶלֶךְ הָעוֹלָם, עַל הַגֶּפֶן וְעַל פְּרִי הַגֶּפֶן,
עַל הָעֵץ וְעַל פְּרִי הָעֵץ:

Baruch atah adonai eloheinu melech ha'olam al hagafen v'al p'ri hagafen, al ha'etz v'al p'ri ha'etz.

Blessed are You, Lord our God, for the vine and its fruit and the tree and its fruit.

May it be Your will that the trees whose fruit we have eaten and blessed will be filled with the strength to flourish and grow during the coming year...for goodness and for blessing, for life and for peace.

In every seed, there is the promise of a new and vital plant. So it is with every child. Each young life holds the promise of a new generation.

לְשָׁנָה טוֹבָה וּבְרָכָה פְּרִי וּתְנוּבָה!

L'SHANAH TOVAH U'VERACHA P'RI U'TENUVAH

MAY THE YEAR BE FRUITFUL AND BLESSED!

HINEI MAH TOV

Psalm 133:1

Folk song

Round

Hi - né ma tov u - ma na - im she-vet a - chim gam ya - chad

II

hi - né ma___ tov u - ma na - im___

D.C.

she - vet a - chim she-vet a - chim gam ya - chad

ARTZA ALINU

Folk tune

Hora

Dm   Gm   Dm   Am   Dm

Ar - tsa a - li - nu ar - tsa a - li - nu ar - tsa a - li - nu

F   C7   F   F   C7   F

k'var cha-rash-nu v'-gam za-ra-nu k'var cha-rash-nu v'-gam za-ra-nu

Gm   Dm   Am   Dm

a - val ōd lō ka - tsar - nu a - val ōd lō ka - tsar - nu

TZADIK KATAMAR

Psalm 92

A. Maslo

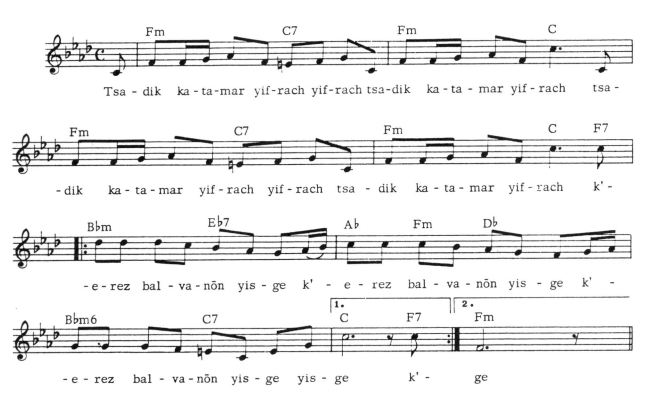

Tsa - dik ka - ta-mar yif-rach yif-rach tsa-dik ka - ta - mar yif - rach tsa-

-dik ka - ta - mar yif - rach yif - rach tsa - dik ka - ta - mar yif - rach k'-

-e - rez bal - va-nōn yis - ge k' - e - rez bal - va-nōn yis - ge k' -

-e - rez bal - va-nōn yis - ge yis - ge k' - ge

HASHKEDIYA

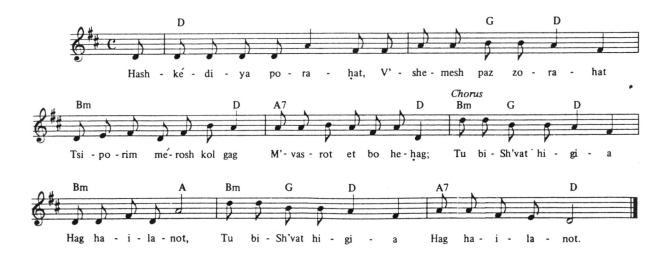

Hash - ké - di - ya po - ra - ḥat, V' - she - mesh paz zo - ra - hat

Tsi - po - rim mé - rosh kol gag M' - vas - rot et bo he - ḥag; Tu bi - Sh'vat hi - gi - a

Hag ha - i - la - not, Tu bi - Sh'vat hi - gi - a Hag ha - i - la - not.

GARDEN SONG

Words and Music by David Mallet

Inch by inch, row by row, gon-na make this gar-den grow,

All it takes is a rake and a hoe and a piece of fer-tile ground.

Inch by inch, row by row, Some-one bless these seeds I sow,

Some-one warm them from be-low 'til the rain comes tum-bl-in

down.

OTHER ACTIVITIES

SING DOWN

Divide into groups, and give each one time to jot down songs with the names of trees, plants, or flowers. Groups take turns singing their songs (no repeats!), and the last group still singing is the winner.

TZEDAKAH BANK

Use this "watering can" for the tzedakah part of the seder. Cover a coffee can with colored paper. Glue a flexible straw to the side and a button to the end of the straw to form the spout. Cut a slit in the plastic lid, large enough for coins.

CREATIVE WRITING

Invite participants to submit their own poems and readings on the themes of trees, nature, and ecology. Use them at the seder.

SEED GRAB-BAG CENTERPIECE

Use for the planting part of the seder. Gather as many packets of vegetable or flower seeds as you have participants. Tie a colorful piece of yarn around each one. Put the seeds in a decorated paper bag with the strings hanging out. Tie another string loosely around the bag. Paste a paper fruit or vegetable to the end of each string. Let each guest pull a string from the grab bag to select seeds to plant.

FAMILY TREES

Have participants draw, bring, and talk about their family trees. Discuss why we use the tree to show our ancestry.

FRUIT FONDUE

In a pot, combine 12 oz. chocolate chips, 1 c. light corn syrup, 2 tsp. vanilla, and a dash of salt. Set on a low flame and stir until smooth. Transfer to a chafing dish or fondue pot. Dip cut up fruit from your seder plates, cake cubes, and marshmallows into the melted chocolate.